Ladybird books are widely available, but in case of difficulty may be ordered by post or telephone from:

Ladybird Books – Cash Sales Department Littlegate Road Paignton Devon TQ3 3BE
Telephone 01803 554761

A catalogue record for this book is available from the British Library

Published by Ladybird Books Ltd Loughborough Leicestershire UK
Ladybird Books Inc Auburn Maine 04210 USA

Telephone TED

by Joan Stimson
illustrated by Peter Stevenson

Picture
Ladybird

The Teddy at Number Ten was bored.
His owner had just started school.
And Ted had too much time on his paws.

Brring, brring. Ted waited for Charlie's
mum to answer the phone. But the
washing machine was going flat out.
And she couldn't hear it.

Brring, brring…
Ted peeked round
the door.

Brring, brring…
he clambered
onto a chair.

And then…
brring, brring…
Ted picked up
the receiver!

"It's only me," said a cheerful voice. "I'd like to pop round after school and bring a cake."

Ted listened eagerly. Then he took a deep breath:

"Hi there, Grandma, that sounds great,
But what a shame I'll have to wait.
Is it chocolate? Is it coffee?
I LOVED the one with lumps of toffee."

But all Grandma heard was a grumbly growl. So she decided to ring back later.

The next day, as soon as
Mum left with Charlie,
the phone rang again.

Brring, brring...
Ted waited for a
few seconds.

Brring, brring...
then he picked it up.

"It's only me," said a cheerful voice.
"Can I borrow Charlie's paints?
I want to make a birthday card."

Ted listened eagerly. Then he
took a deep breath:

"WOW! Brenda, painting's fun,
Especially when the colours run.
Come round tonight and
  don't forget.
We'll ALL try out
  the painting set."

But all Brenda heard was
a grumbly growl. So she
decided to ring back later.

One morning, Mum put up a new shelf. *Wheeee, whirr, whirr, wheeee!* went the electric drill.

Brring, brring… went the phone. And this time Ted picked it up straight away.

"It's only me," said a cheerful voice. "Your motorbike has been repaired, and is ready for collection."

"*Brrmm! Brrmm!*" replied Ted eagerly. Then he took a deep breath:

"I bet it goes just like a rocket,
I'd love to ride in someone's pocket.
I've never tried a motorbike,
But I'm an ace on Charlie's trike."

But all the mechanic heard was a grumbly growl.
So he decided to ring back later.

By now Ted was fed up.
"I wish I could have a
PROPER telephone
conversation!" he sighed.

Brring, brring...
it was well into
the afternoon.

Brring, brring...
Charlie wasn't home
from school.

Brring, brring… and Mum had gone out in her best skirt.

Brring, brring… "Oh, go away," growled Ted.

Brring, brring… "You won't understand a word I say," he grumbled.

Brring, brring, brring, brring… on and on the phone rang.

Until, in the end, Ted snatched it up. And this time he spoke first:

"*I've had a really rotten day,*
  THEY'RE ALL OUT, so I can't play.
I need a chat, I'm all alone,
But no one LISTENS on the phone."

But someone WAS listening.
In fact, the caller heard every single word!

The caller took a
deep breath and
then he replied:

"I'm Brenda's bear from Number Three,
If you stretch up, then you can see,
I'm waving on the window ledge.
It's brilliant now they've cut the hedge."

"I've got some news, it's really great!
I had to tell, I couldn't wait.
Charlie's been here, did you know?
Sorry, Ted, I've got to go…"

Ted looked across the street in amazement.
He could just see Brenda's bear in the window.
Then Charlie and Mum came hurrying home.

"I can't wait to tell Grandma," cried Mum. And
she dived for the phone. As soon as Grandma
answered, Mum squealed with excitement:

"I got it! I got it! I got the lovely hospital job."

"Oh, NO!" groaned Ted. "Now I'll be
on my own EVEN MORE!"

But Ted was wrong.

Because, when Mum went to work, Brenda's mum became Charlie's childminder. She became Ted's bearcarer too! And Ted began to spend his days with Brenda's bear.

Somehow the two friends never ran out of conversation. And, if ever they missed each other when Ted went home… *brring, brring…*

THERE WAS ALWAYS THE PHONE!

Picture Ladybird

Books for reading aloud with 2–6 year olds

The *Picture Ladybird* range is full of exciting stories and rhymes that are perfect to read aloud and share. There is something for everyone – animal stories, bedtime stories, rhyming stories – and lots more!

Ten titles for you to collect

WISHING MOON AGE 3+
written & illustrated by Lesley Harker

Persephone Brown wanted to be BIG. All she ever saw were feet and knees – it really wasn't on. Then one special night her wish came true. Persephone Brown just grew and grew and *GREW*...

DON'T WORRY WILLIAM AGE 3+
by Christine Morton
illustrated by Nigel McMullen

It's a sleepy dark night. A creepy dark night. A night for naughty bears to creep downstairs and have an adventure. But, going in search of biscuits to make them brave, Horace and William hear a bang – a very loud bang – an On-The-Stairs bang! Whatever can it be?

BENEDICT GOES TO THE BEACH AGE 3+
written & illustrated by Chris Demarest

It's hot in the city – *really* hot. Poor Benedict just *has* to cool off. There is only one thing for it, head for the beach – *any* beach! Deciding is the easy part – getting there is another matter altogether...

TOOT! LEARNS TO FLY AGE 3+
by Geraldine Taylor & Jill Harker
illustrated by Georgien Overwater

It's time for Toot to learn to fly, to try and zoom across the sky. First there's take off – watch it – steady! Whoops! Bump! He's not quite ready! Follow Toot's route across the sky and see if he ever *does* learn to fly!

JOE AND THE FARM GOOSE AGE 2+
by Geraldine Taylor & Jill Harker
illustrated by Jakki Wood

A perfect way to introduce young children to farmyard life. There is lots to see and talk about – pigs and their piglets, cows and sheep, hens in the barn – and Joe's special friend – a very inquisitive goose!

THE STAR THAT FELL AGE 3+
by Karen Hayles
illustrated by Cliff Wright

When a star falls from the night sky, Fox and all the other animals want its precious warmth and brightness. When Dog finds the star he gives it to his friend Maddy. But as Maddy's dad tells her, all stars belong to the sky, and soon she must give it back.

TELEPHONE TED AGE 3+
by Joan Stimson
illustrated by Peter Stevenson

When Charlie starts playgroup poor Ted is left sitting at home like a stuffed toy. It's not much fun being a teddy on your own with no one to talk to. But then – *brring, brring* – the telephone rings, and that's when Ted's adventure begins.

JASPER'S JUNGLE JOURNEY AGE 3+
written & illustrated by Val Biro

What's behind those rugged rocks? A lion wearing purple socks! Just one of the strange sights Jasper encounters as he goes in search of his lost teddy bear. A delightful rhyming story full of jungle surprises!

SHOO FLY SHOO! AGE 4+
by Brian Moses
illustrated by Trevor Dunton

If a fly flies by and it's bothering you, just swish it and swash it and tell it to *shoo!* Trace the trail of the buzzing, zuzzing fly in this gloriously silly rhyming story.

GOING TO PLAYGROUP AGE 2+
by Geraldine Taylor & Jill Harker
illustrated by Terry McKenna

Tom's day at playgroup is full of exciting activities. He's a cook, a mechanic, a pirate and a band leader... he even flies to the moon! Ideal for children starting playgroup and full of ideas for having fun at home, too!